MR. POPPER'S
PENGUINS

MR. POPPER'S PENGUINS

by
Richard and Florence Atwater

Illustrated by Robert Lawson

A Yearling Book

Published by
Dell Publishing Co., Inc.
1 Dag Hammarskjold Plaza
New York, New York 10017

Yearling ® TM 913705, Dell Publishing Co., Inc.

ISBN: 0-440-45934-6

Reprinted by arrangement with Little, Brown and Company (Inc.)

Printed in the United States of America

One Previous Yearling Edition

October 1986

10 9 8 7 6 5 4 3 2 1

CW

Contents

MR. POPPER'S PENGUINS

CHAPTER I

Stillwater

IT WAS AN afternoon in late September. In the pleasant little city of Stillwater, Mr. Popper, the house painter, was going home from work.

He was carrying his buckets, his ladders, and his boards so that he had rather a hard time moving along. He was spattered here and there with paint and calcimine, and there were bits of wallpaper clinging to his hair and whiskers, for he was rather an untidy man.

The children looked up from their play to smile at him

3

as he passed, and the housewives, seeing him, said, "Oh dear, there goes Mr. Popper. I must remember to ask John to have the house painted over in the spring."

4

No one knew what went on inside of Mr. Popper's head, and no one guessed that he would one day be the most famous person in Stillwater.

He was a dreamer. Even when he was busiest smoothing down the paste on the wallpaper, or painting the outside of other people's houses, he would forget what he was doing. Once he had painted three sides of a kitchen green, and the other side yellow. The housewife, instead of being angry and making him do it over, had liked it so well that she had made him leave it that way. And all the other housewives, when they saw it, admired it too, so that pretty soon everybody in Stillwater had two-colored kitchens.

The reason Mr. Popper was so absent-minded was that he was always dreaming about far-away countries. He had never been out of Stillwater. Not that he was unhappy. He had a nice little house of his own, a wife whom he loved dearly, and two children, named Janie and Bill. Still, it would have been nice, he often thought, if he could have seen something of the world before he met Mrs. Popper and settled down. He had never hunted tigers in India, or climbed the peaks of the Himalayas, or dived for pearls in the South Seas. Above all, he had never seen the Poles.

That was what he regretted most of all. He had never seen those great shining white expanses of ice and snow. How he wished that he had been a scientist, instead of a house painter in Stillwater, so that he might have joined some of the great Polar expeditions. Since he could not go, he was always thinking about them.

Whenever he heard that a Polar movie was in town, he was the first person at the ticket-window, and often he sat through three shows. Whenever the town library had a new book about the Arctic or the Antarctic — the North Pole or the South Pole — Mr. Popper was the first to borrow it. Indeed, he had read so much about Polar explorers that he could name all of them and tell you what each had done. He was quite an authority on the subject.

His evenings were the best time of all. Then he could sit down in his little house and read about those cold regions at the top and bottom of the earth. As he read he could take the little globe that Janie and Bill had given him the Christmas before, and search out the exact spot he was reading about.

So now, as he made his way through the streets, he was happy because the day was over, and because it was the end of September.

When he came to the gate of the neat little bungalow at 432 Proudfoot Avenue, he turned in.

"Well, my love," he said, setting down his buckets and ladders and boards, and kissing Mrs. Popper, "the decorating season is over. I have painted all the kitchens in Stillwater; I have papered all the rooms in the new apartment building on Elm Street. There is no more work until spring, when people will want their houses painted."

Mrs. Popper sighed. "I sometimes wish you had the kind of work that lasted all year, instead of just from spring until fall," she said. "It will be very nice to have you at home for a vacation, of course, but it is a little hard to sweep with a man sitting around reading all day."

"I could decorate the house for you."

"No, indeed," said Mrs. Popper firmly. "Last year you painted the bathroom four different times, because you had nothing else to do, and I think that is enough of that. But what worries me is the money. I have saved a little, and I daresay we can get along as we have other winters. No more roast beef, no more ice cream, not even on Sundays."

"Shall we have beans every day?" asked Janie and Bill, coming in from play.

"I'm afraid so," said Mrs. Popper. "Anyway, go wash your hands, for supper. And Papa, put away this litter of paints, because you won't be needing them for quite a while."

CHAPTER II

The Voice in the Air

THAT EVENING, when the little Poppers had been put to bed, Mr. and Mrs. Popper settled down for a long, quiet evening. The neat living room at 432 Proudfoot Avenue was much like all the other living rooms in Stillwater, except that the walls were hung with pictures from the *National Geographic Magazine*. Mrs. Popper picked up her mending, while Mr. Popper collected his pipe, his book, and his globe.

9

From time to time Mrs. Popper sighed a little as she thought about the long winter ahead. Would there really be enough beans to last, she wondered.

Mr. Popper was not worried, however. As he put on his spectacles, he was quite pleased at the prospect of a whole winter of reading travel books, with no work to interrupt him. He set his little globe beside him and began to read.

"What are you reading?" asked Mrs. Popper.

"I am reading a book called *Antarctic Adventures*. It is very interesting. It tells all about the different people who have gone to the South Pole and what they have found there."

"Don't you ever get tired of reading about the South Pole?"

"No, I don't. Of course I would much rather go there than read about it. But reading is the next best thing."

"I think it must be very boring down there," said Mrs. Popper. "It sounds very dull and cold, with all that ice and snow."

"Oh, no," answered Mr. Popper. "You wouldn't think it was dull if you had gone with me to see the movies of the Drake Expedition at the Bijou last year."

"Well, I didn't, and I don't think any of us will have any money for movies now," answered Mrs. Popper, a little sharply. She was not at all a disagreeable woman, but she sometimes got rather cross when she was worried about money.

"If you had gone, my love," went on Mr. Popper, "you would have seen how beautiful the Antarctic is. But I think the nicest part of all is the penguins. No wonder all the men on that expedition had such a good time playing with them. They are the funniest birds in the world. They don't fly like other birds. They walk erect like little men. When they get tired of walking they just lie down on their stomachs and slide. It would be very nice to have one for a pet."

"Pets!" said Mrs. Popper. "First it's Bill wanting a dog and then Janie begging for a kitten. Now you and penguins! But I won't have any pets around. They make

11

too much dirt in the house, and I have enough work now, trying to keep this place tidy. To say nothing of what it costs to feed a pet. Anyway, we have the bowl of gold-fish."

"Penguins are very intelligent," continued Mr. Popper. "Listen to this, Mamma. It says here that when they want to catch some shrimps, they all crowd over to the edge of an ice bank. Only they don't just jump in, because a sea leopard might be waiting to eat the penguins. So they crowd and push until they manage to shove one penguin off, to see if it's safe. I mean if he doesn't get eaten up, the rest of them know it's safe for them all to jump in."

"Dear me!" said Mrs. Popper in a shocked tone. "They sound to me like pretty heathen birds."

"It's a queer thing," said Mr. Popper, "that all the polar bears live at the North Pole and all the penguins at the South Pole. I should think the penguins would like the North Pole, too, if they only knew how to get there."

At ten o'clock Mrs. Popper yawned and laid down her

mending. "Well, you can go on reading about those heathen birds, but I am going to bed. Tomorrow is Thursday, September thirtieth, and I have to go to the first meeting of the Ladies' Aid and Missionary Society."

"September thirtieth!" said Mr. Popper in an excited tone. "You don't mean that tonight is Wednesday, September twenty-ninth?"

"Why, yes, I suppose it is. But what of it?"

Mr. Popper put down his book of *Antarctic Adventures* and moved hastily to the radio.

"What of it!" he repeated, pushing the switch. "Why, this is the night the Drake Antarctic Expedition is going to start broadcasting."

"That's nothing," said Mrs. Popper. "Just a lot of men at the bottom of the world saying 'Hello, Mamma. Hello, Papa.'"

"*Sh!*" commanded Mr. Popper, laying his ear close to the radio.

There was a buzz, and then suddenly, from the South Pole, a faint voice floated out into the Popper living room.

"This is Admiral Drake speaking. Hello, Mamma. Hello, Papa. Hello, Mr. Popper."

"Gracious goodness," exclaimed Mrs. Popper. "Did he say 'Papa' or 'Popper'?"

"Hello, Mr. Popper, up there in Stillwater. Thanks for your nice letter about the pictures of our last expedition. Watch for an answer. But not by letter, Mr. Popper. Watch for a surprise. Signing off. Signing off."

"*You* wrote to Admiral Drake?"

"Yes, I did," Mr. Popper admitted. "I wrote and told him how funny I thought the penguins were."

"Well, I never," said Mrs. Popper, very much impressed.

Mr. Popper picked up his little globe and found the Antarctic. "And to think he spoke to me all the way from there. And he even mentioned my name. Mamma, what do you suppose he means by a surprise?"

"I haven't any idea," answered Mrs. Popper, "but I'm going to bed. I don't want to be late for the Ladies' Aid and Missionary Society meeting tomorrow."

CHAPTER III

Out of the Antarctic

WHAT WITH THE excitement of having the great Admiral Drake speak to him over the radio, and his curiosity about the Admiral's message to him, Mr. Popper did not sleep very well that night. He did not see how he could possibly wait to find out what the Admiral meant. When morning came, he was almost sorry that he had nowhere to go, no houses to paint, no rooms to paper. It would have helped to pass the time.

"Would you like the living room papered over?" he

asked Mrs. Popper. "I have quite a lot of Paper Number 88, left over from the Mayor's house."

"I would not," said Mrs. Popper firmly. "The paper on now is plenty good enough. I am going to the first meeting of the Ladies' Aid and Missionary Society today and I don't want any mess around to clean up when I get home."

"Very well, my love," said Mr. Popper meekly, and he settled down with his pipe, his globe, and his book of *Antarctic Adventures*. But somehow, as he read today, he could not keep his mind on the printed words. His thoughts kept straying away to Admiral Drake. What could he have meant by a surprise for Mr. Popper?

Fortunately for his peace of mind, he did not have so very long to wait. That afternoon, while Mrs. Popper was still away at her meeting, and Janie and Bill had not yet come home from school, there was a loud ring at the front door.

"I suppose it is just the postman. I won't bother to answer it," he said to himself.

The bell rang again, a little louder this time. Grumbling to himself, Mr. Popper went to the door.

It was not the postman who stood there. It was an expressman with the largest box Mr. Popper had ever seen.

"Party by the name of Popper live here?"

"That's me."

"Well, here's a package that's come Air Express all the way from Antarctica. Some journey, I'll say."

Mr. Popper signed the receipt and examined the box. It was covered all over with markings. "UNPACK AT ONCE," said one. "KEEP COOL," said another. He noticed that the box was punched here and there with air holes.

You can imagine that once he had the box inside the house, Mr. Popper lost no time in getting the screw driver, for by this time, of course, he had guessed that it was the surprise from Admiral Drake.

He had succeeded in removing the outer boards and part of the packing, which was a layer of dry ice, when from the depths of the packing case he suddenly heard a faint "*Ork*." His heart stood still. Surely he had heard that sound before at the Drake Expedition movies. His hands were trembling so that he could scarcely lift off the last of the wrappings.

There was not the slightest doubt about it. It was a penguin.

Mr. Popper was speechless with delight.

But the penguin was not speechless. "*Ork,*" it said again, and this time it held out its flippers and jumped over the packing debris.

It was a stout little fellow about two and a half feet high. Although it was about the size of a small child, it looked much more like a little gentleman, with its smooth white waistcoat in front and its long black tailcoat dragging a little behind. Its eyes were set in two white circles in its black head. It turned its head from one side to the other, as first with one eye and then with the other, it examined Mr. Popper.

Mr. Popper had read that penguins are extremely curious, and he soon found that this was true, for stepping out, the visitor began to inspect the house. Down the hall

it went and into the bedrooms, with its strange, pompous little strut. When it, or he — Mr. Popper had already begun to think of it as he — got to the bathroom, it looked around with a pleased expression on its face.

"Perhaps," thought Mr. Popper, "all that white tiling reminds him of the ice and snow at the South Pole. Poor thing, maybe he's thirsty."

Carefully Mr. Popper began to fill the bathtub with cold water. This was a little difficult because the inquisitive bird kept reaching over and trying to bite the faucets with its sharp red beak. Finally, however, he succeeded in getting the tub all filled. Since the penguin kept looking over, Mr. Popper picked it up and dropped it in. The penguin seemed not to mind.

"Anyway, you're not shy," said Mr. Popper. "I guess you've got sort of used to playing around with those explorers at the Pole."

When he thought the penguin had had enough of a bath, he drew out the stopper. He was just wondering what to do next when Janie and Bill burst in from school.

"Papa," they shouted together at the bathroom door. "What is it?"

"It's a South Pole penguin sent to me by Admiral Drake."

"Look!" said Bill. "It's marching."

The delighted penguin was indeed marching. With little pleased nods of his handsome black head he was parading up and down the inside of the bathtub. Sometimes he seemed to be counting the steps it took — six steps for the length, two steps for the width, six steps for the length again, and two more for the width.

"For such a big bird he takes awfully small steps," said Bill.

"And look how his little black coat drags behind. It almost looks as if it were too big for him," said Janie.

But the penguin was tired of marching. This time, when it got to the end of the tub, it decided to jump up the slippery curve. Then it turned, and with outstretched flippers, tobogganed down on its white stomach. They could see that those flippers, which were black on the outside, like the sleeves of a tailcoat, were white underneath.

"*Gook! Gook!*" said the penguin, trying its new game again and again.

"What's his name, Papa?" asked Janie.

"*Gook! Gook!*" said the penguin, sliding down once more on his glossy white stomach.

"It sounds something like 'Cook,'" said Mr. Popper. "Why, that's it, of course. We'll call him Cook — Captain Cook."

CHAPTER IV

Captain Cook

CALL WHO Captain Cook?" asked Mrs. Popper, who had come in so quietly that none of them had heard her.

"Why, the penguin," said Mr. Popper. "I was just saying," he went on, as Mrs. Popper sat down suddenly on the floor to recover from her surprise, "that we'd name him after Captain Cook. He was a famous English explorer who lived about the time of the American Revolution. He sailed all over where no one had ever been before. He didn't actually get to the

South Pole, of course, but he made a lot of important scientific discoveries about the Antarctic regions. He was a brave man and a kind leader. So I think Captain Cook would be a very suitable name for our penguin here."

"Well, I never!" said Mrs. Popper.

"*Gork!*" said Captain Cook, suddenly getting lively again. With a flap of his flippers he jumped from the tub to the washstand, and stood there for a minute surveying the floor. Then he jumped down, walked over to Mrs. Popper, and began to peck her ankle.

"Stop him, Papa!" screamed Mrs. Popper, retreating into the hallway with Captain Cook after her, and Mr. Popper and the children following. In the living room she paused. So did Captain Cook, for he was delighted with the room.

Now a penguin may look very strange in a living room, but a living room looks very strange to a penguin. Even Mrs. Popper had to smile as they watched Captain Cook, with the light of curiosity in his excited circular eyes, and his black tailcoat dragging pompously behind his

little pinkish feet, strut from one upholstered chair to another, pecking at each to see what it was made of. Then he turned suddenly and marched out to the kitchen.

"Maybe he's hungry," said Janie.

Captain Cook immediately marched up to the refrigerator.

"*Gork?*" he inquired, turning to slant his head wisely at Mrs. Popper, and looking at her pleadingly with his right eye.

"He certainly is cute," she said. "I guess I'll have to forgive him for biting my ankle. He probably only did it out of curiosity. Anyway, he's a nice clean-looking bird."

"*Ork?*" repeated the penguin, nibbling at the metal handle of the refrigerator door with his upstretched beak.

Mr. Popper opened the door for him, and Captain Cook stood very high and leaned his sleek black head back so that he could see inside. Now that Mr. Popper's work was over for the winter, the icebox was not quite so full as usual, but the penguin did not know that.

"What do you suppose he likes to eat?" asked Mrs. Popper.

"Let's see," said Mr. Popper, as he removed all the

25

food and set it on the kitchen table. "Now then, Captain Cook, take a look."

The penguin jumped up onto a chair and from there onto the edge of the table, flapping his flippers again to recover his balance. Then he walked solemnly around the table, and between the dishes of food, inspecting everything with the greatest interest, though he touched nothing. Finally he stood still, very erect, raised his beak to point at the ceiling, and make a loud, almost purring sound. "*O-r-r-r-h, o-r-r-r-h,*" he trilled.

"That's a penguin's way of saying how pleased it is," said Mr. Popper, who had read about it in his Antarctic books.

Apparently, however, what Captain Cook wanted to show was that he was pleased with their kindness, rather than with their food. For now, to their surprise, he jumped down and walked into the dining room.

"I know," said Mr. Popper. "We ought to have some seafood for him, canned shrimps or something. Or maybe he isn't hungry yet. I've read that penguins can go for a month without food."

"Mamma! Papa!" called Bill. "Come see what Captain Cook has done."

Captain Cook had done it all right. He had discovered the bowl of goldfish on the dining-room window sill. By the time Mrs. Popper reached over to lift him away, he had already swallowed the last of the goldfish.

"Bad, bad penguin!" reproved Mrs. Popper, glaring down at Captain Cook.

Captain Cook squatted guiltily on the carpet and tried to make himself look small.

"He knows he's done wrong," said Mr. Popper. "Isn't he smart?"

"Maybe we can train him," said Mrs. Popper. "Bad, naughty Captain," she said to the penguin in a loud voice. "Bad, to eat the goldfish." And she spanked him on his round black head.

Before she could do that again, Captain Cook hastily waddled out to the kitchen.

There the Poppers found him trying to hide in the still opened refrigerator. He was squatting under the ice-cube coils, under which he could barely squeeze, sitting down. His round, white-circled eyes looked out at them mysteriously from the dimness of the inside of the box.

"I think that's about the right temperature for him, at that," said Mr. Popper. "We could let him sleep there, at night."

"But where will I put the food?" asked Mrs. Popper.

"Oh, I guess we can get another icebox for the food," said Mr. Popper.

"Look," said Janie. "He's gone to sleep."

Mr. Popper turned the cold control switch to its coldest so that Captain Cook could sleep more comfortably. Then he left the door ajar so that the penguin would have plenty of fresh air to breathe.

"Tomorrow I will have the icebox service department send a man out to bore some holes in the door, for air," he said, "and then he can put a handle on the inside of the door so that Captain Cook can go in and out of his refrigerator, as he pleases."

"Well, dear me, I never thought we would have a penguin for a pet," said Mrs. Popper. "Still, he behaves pretty well, on the whole, and he is so nice and clean that perhaps he will be a good example to you and the children. And now, I declare, we must get busy. We haven't done anything but watch that bird. Papa, will you just help me to set the beans on the table, please?"

"Just a minute," answered Mr. Popper. "I just happened to think that Captain Cook will not feel right on the floor of that icebox. Penguins make their nests of pebbles and stones. So I will just take some ice cubes out of the tray and put them under him. That way he will be more comfortable."

CHAPTER V

Troubles with a Penguin

T HE NEXT DAY was quite eventful at 432 Proudfoot Avenue. First there was the service man and then the policeman and then the trouble about the license.

Captain Cook was in the children's room, watching Janie and Bill put together a jigsaw puzzle on the floor. He was very good about not disturbing the pieces after Bill had spanked him for eating one. He did not hear the refrigerator service man come to the back door.

Mrs. Popper had gone marketing for canned shrimps

for the penguin, so that Mr. Popper was alone in the kitchen to explain to the service man what he wanted done to the refrigerator.

The service man put his tool bag down on the kitchen floor, looked at the refrigerator, and then at Mr. Popper, who, to tell the truth, had not shaved yet and was not very tidy.

"Mister," he said, "you don't need no ventilating holes in that there door."

"It's my icebox, and I want some holes bored in the door," said Mr. Popper.

They argued about it for quite a while. Mr. Popper knew that to get the service man to do what he wanted, all he had to do was to explain that he was going to keep a live penguin in the icebox, and that he wanted his pet to have plenty of fresh air, even though the door was closed all night. He felt a little stubborn about explaining, however. He didn't want to discuss Captain Cook with this unsympathetic service man, who was already staring at

Mr. Popper as if he thought Mr. Popper was not quite right in his head.

"Come on, do what I said," said Mr. Popper. "I'm paying you for it."

"With what?" asked the service man.

Mr. Popper gave him a five-dollar bill. It made him a little sad to think how many beans it would have bought for Mrs. Popper and the children.

The service man examined the bill carefully as if he didn't trust Mr. Popper too much. But at last he put it in his pocket, took a drill from his tool bag, and made five small holes in a neat pattern on the refrigerator door.

"Now," said Mr. Popper, "don't get up. Wait a minute. There is one more thing."

"Now what?" said the service man. "I suppose now you want me to take the door off its hinges to let in a little more air. Or do you want me to make a radio set out of your icebox?"

"Don't get funny," said Mr. Popper indignantly. "That

33

is no way to talk. Believe it or not, I know what I'm doing. I mean, having you do. I want you to fix an extra handle on the inside of that box so it can be opened from the inside of the box."

"That," said the service man, "is a fine idea. You want an extra handle on the inside. Sure, sure." He picked up his tool bag.

"Aren't you going to do it for me?" asked Mr. Popper.

"Oh, sure, sure," said the service man, edging toward the back door.

Mr. Popper saw that for all his words of agreement, the service man had no intention of putting on an inside handle.

"I thought you were a service man," he said.

"I am. That's the first sensible thing you've said yet."

"You're a fine kind of service man if you don't even know how to put an extra handle on the inside of an ice-box door."

"Oh, I don't, don't I? Don't think I don't know how. As far as that goes, I've even got a spare handle in my tool bag, and plenty of screws. You needn't think I don't know how to do it, if I wanted to."

Mr. Popper silently reached into his pocket and gave the service man his last five-dollar bill. He was pretty sure that Mrs. Popper would be annoyed at him for spending all that money, but it could not be helped.

"Mister," said the service man, "you win. I'll fix your extra handle. And while I am doing it, you sit down on that chair over there facing me, where I can keep an eye on you."

"Fair enough," said Mr. Popper, sitting down.

The service man was still on the floor, putting in the finals screws that held the new handle in place, when the penguin came out to the kitchen on his silent pink feet.

Surprised at seeing a strange man sitting on the floor, Captain Cook quietly walked over and began to peck him curiously. But the service man was even more surprised than Captain Cook.

"*Ork*," said the penguin. Or perhaps it was the service man. Mr. Popper was not sure just what had happened when he picked up himself and his chair a moment later. There had been a shower of flying tools, a violent slamming of the door, and the service man was gone.

These sudden noises, of course, brought the children running. Mr. Popper showed them how the refrigerator was now all remodeled for the penguin. He showed Captain Cook, too, by shutting him inside it. The penguin at once noticed the shiny new inside handle and bit it with his usual curiosity. The door opened, and Captain Cook jumped out.

Mr. Popper promptly put Captain Cook back inside and shut the door again, to be sure that the penguin learned his lesson. Before long, Captain Cook became quite skillful at getting out and was ready to be taught how to get inside when the door was shut.

By the time the policeman came to the back door, Captain Cook was going in and out the refrigerator as easily as if he had lived in one all his life.

CHAPTER VI

More Troubles

THE CHILDREN were the first to notice the policeman.

"Look, Papa," said Bill. "There's a policeman at the back door. Is he going to arrest you?"

"*Gook*," said Captain Cook, walking with dignity to the door, and trying to poke his beak through the screen.

"Is this 432 Proudfoot Avenue?"

"It is," answered Mr. Popper.

"Well, I guess this is the place all right," said the policeman, and pointed to Captain Cook. "Is that thing yours?"

38

"Yes, it is," said Mr. Popper, proudly.

"And what do you do for a living?" asked the police-man sternly.

"Papa is an artist," said Janie.

"He's always getting paint and calcimine all over his clothes," said Bill.

"I'm a house painter, a decorator," said Mr. Popper. "Won't you come in?"

"I won't," said the policeman, "unless I have to."

"Ha, ha!" said Bill. "The policeman is afraid of Captain Cook."

"*Gaw!*" said the penguin, opening his red beak wide, as if he wanted to laugh at the policeman.

"Can it talk?" asked the policeman. "What is it — a giant parrot?"

"It's a penguin," said Janie. "We keep it for a pet."

"Well, if it's only a bird . . . " said the policeman, lifting his cap to scratch his head in a puzzled sort of way. "From the way that fellow with a tool bag yelled at me outside, I thought there was a lion loose in here."

39

"Mamma says Papa's hair looks like a lion's sometimes," said Bill.

"Keep still, Bill," said Janie. "The policeman doesn't care how Papa's hair looks."

The policeman now scratched his chin. "If it's only a bird, I suppose it will be O. K. if you keep him in a cage."

"We keep him in the icebox," said Bill.

"You can put it in the icebox, for all I care," said the policeman. "What kind of a bird did you say it was?"

"A penguin," answered Mr. Popper. "And by the way, I might want to take him walking with me. Would it be all right, if I kept him on a leash?"

"I tell you," said the policeman, "honestly I don't know what the municipal ordinance about penguins is, with or without a leash, on the public streets. I'll ask my sergeant."

"Maybe I ought to get a license for him," suggested Mr. Popper.

"It's certainly big enough for a license," said the policeman. "I tell you what to do. You call up the City Hall and ask them what the ruling about penguins is. And good luck to you, Popper. He's kind of a cute little fellow, at that. Looks almost human. Good day to you, Popper, and good day to you, Mr. Penguin."

When Mr. Popper telephoned the City Hall to see about a license for Captain Cook, the penguin did his best to disconnect the telephone by biting the green cord. Perhaps he thought it was some new kind of eel. But just then Mrs. Popper came back from market and opened a can of shrimps, so that Mr. Popper was soon left alone at the telephone.

Even so, he found it was not so easy to learn whether or not he must get a license for his strange pet. Every time he would explain what he wanted, he would be told to wait a minute, and much later a new voice would ask him what he wanted. This went on for considerable time. At last a new voice seemed to take a little interest in the case. Pleased with this friendly voice, Mr. Popper began again to tell about Captain Cook.

"Is he an army captain, a police captain, or a navy captain?"

"He is not," said Mr. Popper. "He's a penguin."

"Will you repeat that, please?" said the voice.

Mr. Popper repeated it. The voice suggested that perhaps he had better spell it.

"P-e-n-g-u-i-n," said Mr. Popper. "Penguin."

"Oh!" said the voice. "You mean that Captain Cook's first name is Benjamin?"

"Not Benjamin. Penguin. It's a bird," said Mr. Popper.

"Do you mean," said the phone in his ear, "that Captain Cook wishes a license to shoot birds? I am sorry. The bird-hunting season does not open until November. And please try to speak a little more distinctly, Mr. — Topper, did you say your name is?"

"My name is Popper, not Topper," shouted Mr. Popper.

"Yes, Mr. Potter. Now I can hear you quite clearly."

"Then listen," roared Mr. Popper, now completely outraged. "If you folks at the City Hall don't even know what penguins are, I guess you haven't any rule saying they have to be licensed. I will do without a license for Captain Cook."

"Just a minute, Mr. Popwell. Our own Mr. Tread-bottom of the Bureau of Navigation of Lakes, Rivers, Ponds, and Streams, has just come in. I will let you speak to him personally. Perhaps he knows this Benjamin Cook of yours."

In a moment a new voice was speaking to Mr. Popper. "Good morning. This is the Automobile License Bureau. Did you have this same car last year, and if so, what was the license number?"

Mr. Popper had been switched over to the County Building.

He decided to hang up.

CHAPTER VII

Captain Cook Builds
A Nest

VERY RELUCTANTLY, Janie and
Bill had to leave Captain Cook and
go to school. Mrs. Popper was busy in
the kitchen, rather belatedly doing the
breakfast dishes; and while she dimly
realized that the penguin was going in and out the refrigerator pretty frequently, she thought nothing of it
at first.

Meanwhile Mr. Popper had abandoned his telephon-
ing and was now busy shaving and making himself neat
in honor of being the owner of such a splendid bird as
Captain Cook.

44

But the penguin, though thus neglected for the moment, was by no means idle.

With the unusual excitement, and having to go to market earlier than usual, Mrs. Popper had not yet got around to straightening the house. She was an excellent housekeeper. Still, with two children like Janie and Bill and a husband with such untidy ways, there is no denying the fact that she had to pick up the place rather frequently.

Captain Cook was now attending to the picking up.

Into the corners of every room he prowled and poked and pecked with a busy thoroughness; into every closet he stared with his white-circled eyes; under and behind all the furniture he crowded his plump figure, with little subdued cries of curiosity, surprise, and pleasure.

And each time he found what he seemed to be looking for, he picked it up in the black end of his red beak, and carried it, waddling proudly on his wide, pink feet, into the kitchen, and into the icebox.

At last it occurred to Mrs. Popper to wonder what on

earth the busy bird was up to. When she looked, she could only scream to Mr. Popper to come quickly and see what Captain Cook had done now.

Mr. Popper, himself looking rather remarkable, as Mrs. Popper noticed later, joined her in staring with astonishment into the refrigerator.

Captain Cook came up, too, and helped them look.
"*Ork, ork,*" he said with triumph.

Mrs. Popper laughed, and Mr. Popper gasped as they
saw the results of Captain Cook's trips through the
house.

Two spools of thread, one white chess bishop, and six

parts of a jigsaw puzzle . . . A teaspoon and a closed box of safety matches . . . A radish, two pennies, a nickel, and a golf ball. Two pencil stubs, one bent playing card, and a small ash tray.

Five hairpins, an olive, two dominoes, and a sock . . . A nailfile, four buttons of various sizes, a telephone slug, seven marbles, and a tiny doll's chair . . .

Five checker pieces, a bit of graham cracker, a parchesi cup, and an eraser . . . A door key, a buttonhook, and a crumpled piece of tinfoil . . . Half of a very old lemon, the head of a china doll, Mr. Popper's pipe, and a ginger-ale cap . . . An inkbottle cork, two screws, and a belt buckle . . .

Six beads from a child's necklace, five building blocks, a darning egg, a bone, a small harmonica, and a partly consumed lollipop. Two toothpaste lids and a small red notebook.

"I guess this is what you call the rookery," said Mr. Popper. "Only he couldn't find any stones to build his nest with."

"Well," said Mrs. Popper, "those penguins may have

heathen ways at the South Pole, but I declare I think this one is going to be quite a help around the house."

"*Ork!*" said Captain Cook, and strutting into the living room, he knocked over the best lamp.

"I think, Papa," said Mrs. Popper, "that you had better take Captain Cook outside for a little exercise. Good gracious, but you're all dressed up. Why, you look almost like a penguin yourself."

Mr. Popper had smoothed down his hair and shaved off his whiskers. Never again would Mrs. Popper have to reproach him for looking as wild as a lion. He had put on a white shirt with a white tie and white flannel trousers, and a pair of bright tan, oxblood shoes. He had got out of the cedar chest his old black evening tailcoat, that he had been married in, and brushed it carefully, and put it on, too.

He did indeed look a little like a penguin. He turned and strutted like one now, for Mrs. Popper.

But he did not forget his duty to Captain Cook.

"Can I have a few yards of clothesline, please, Mamma?" asked Mr. Popper.

CHAPTER VIII

Penguin's Promenade

M R. POPPER soon found that it was not so easy to take a penguin for a stroll.

Captain Cook did not care at first for the idea of being put on a leash. However, Mr. Popper was firm. He tied one end of the clothesline to the penguin's fat throat and the other to his own wrist.

"*Ork!*" said Captain Cook indignantly. Still, he was a very reasonable sort of bird, and when he saw that protesting did him no good, he recovered his customary dignity and decided to let Mr. Popper lead him.

Mr. Popper put on his best Sunday derby and opened the front door with Captain Cook waddling graciously beside him.

"*Gaw,*" said the penguin, stopping at the edge of the porch to look down at the steps.

Mr. Popper gave him plenty of clothesline leash.

"*Gook!*" said Captain Cook, and raising his flippers, he leaned forward bravely and tobogganed down the steps on his stomach.

Mr. Popper followed, though not in the same way. Captain Cook quickly got up on his feet again and strutted to the street ahead of Mr. Popper with many quick turns of his head and pleased comments on the new scene.

Down Proudfoot Avenue came a neighbor of the Poppers, Mrs. Callahan, with her arms full of groceries. She stared in astonishment when she saw Captain Cook and Mr. Popper, looking like a larger penguin himself in his black tailcoat.

"Heavens have mercy on us!" she exclaimed as the

bird began to investigate the striped stockings under her house dress. "It isn't an owl and it isn't a goose."

"It isn't," said Mr. Popper, tipping his Sunday derby. "It's an Antarctic penguin, Mrs. Callahan."

"Get away from me," said Mrs. Callahan to Captain Cook. "An anteater, is it?"

"Not anteater," explained Mr. Popper. "Antarctic. It was sent to me from the South Pole."

"Take your South Pole goose away from me at once," said Mrs. Callahan.

Mr. Popper pulled obediently at the clothesline, while Captain Cook took a parting peck at Mrs. Callahan's striped stockings.

"Heaven preserve us!" said Mrs. Callahan. "I must stop in and see Mrs. Popper at once. I would never have believed it. I will be going now."

"So will I," said Mr. Popper as Captain Cook dragged him off down the street.

Their next stop was at the drugstore at the corner of Proudfoot Avenue and Main Street. Here Captain Cook

insisted on looking over the window display, which consisted of several open packages of shiny white boric crystals. These he evidently mistook for polar snow, for he began to peck at the window vigorously.

Suddenly a car wheeled to the near-by curb with a shriek of its brakes, and two young men sprang out, one of them bearing a camera.

"This must be it," said the first young man to the other.

"It's them, all right," said the second young man.

The cameraman set up his tripod on the sidewalk. By this time a small crowd had gathered around, and two men in white coats had even come out of the drugstore to watch. Captain Cook, however, was still too much interested in the window exhibits to bother to turn around.

"You're Mr. Popper of 432 Proudfoot Avenue, aren't you?" asked the second young man, pulling a notebook out of his pocket.

"Yes," said Mr. Popper, realizing that his picture was

about to be taken for the newspaper. The two young men had, as a matter of fact, heard about the strange bird from the policeman, and had been on their way to the Popper house, to get an interview, when they saw Captain Cook.

"Hey, pelican, turn around and see the pretty birdie," said the photographer.

"That's no pelican," said the other, who was a reporter. "Pelicans have a pouch in their bills."

"I'd think it was a dodo, only dodos are extinct. This will make an elegant picture, if I can ever get her to turn around."

"It's a penguin," said Mr. Popper proudly. "Its name is Captain Cook."

"*Gook!*" said the penguin, turning around, now that they were talking about him. Spying the camera tripod, he walked over and examined it.

"Probably thinks it's a three-legged stork," said the photographer.

"This bird of yours — " said the reporter. "Is it a he or a she? The public will want to know."

Mr. Popper hesitated. "Well, I call it Captain Cook."

"That makes it a he," said the reporter, writing rapidly in his notebook.

Still curious, Captain Cook started walking round and round the tripod, till the clothesline, the penguin, Mr. Popper and the tripod were all tangled up. At the advice of one of the bystanders, the tangle was finally straightened out by Mr. Popper's walking around the tripod three times in the opposite direction. At last, Captain Cook, standing still beside Mr. Popper, consented to pose.

Mr. Popper straightened his tie, and the cameraman snapped the picture. Captain Cook shut his eyes, and this is the way his picture appeared later in all the newspapers.

"One last question," said the reporter. "Where did you get your strange pet?"

"From Admiral Drake, the South Pole explorer. He sent him to me for a present."

"Yeah," said the reporter. "Anyway, it's a good story."

The two young men jumped into their car. Mr. Popper and Captain Cook continued their walk, with quite a crowd following and asking questions. The crowd was getting so thick that, in order to escape, Mr. Popper led Captain Cook into a barbershop.

The man who kept the barbershop had, up to this time, been a very good friend of Mr. Popper's.

CHAPTER IX

In the Barber Shop

I T WAS very quiet in the barbershop. The barber was shaving an elderly gentleman.

Captain Cook found this spectacle very interesting, and in order to get a better view, he jumped up on the mirror ledge.

"Good night!" said the barber.

The gentleman in the barber's chair, his face already white with lather, half-lifted his head to see what had happened.

"*Gook!*" said the penguin, flapping his flippers and

reaching out his long beak toward the lather on the
gentleman's face.

58

With a yell and a leap, the gentleman rose from his re-clining position, left the barber's chair, and fled into the street, not even stopping for his coat and hat.

"*Gaw!*" said Captain.

"Hey," said the barber to Mr. Popper. "Take that thing out of my shop. This is no zoo. What's the idea?"

"Do you mind if I take him out your back door?" asked Mr. Popper.

"Any door," said the barber, "as long as it's quick. Now it's biting the teeth off my combs."

Mr. Popper took Captain Cook in his arms, and amid cries of "*Quork?*" "*Gawk!*" and "*Ork!*" made his way out of the shop and its back room and out a door into an alley.

Captain Cook now discovered his first back stairway.

Mr. Popper discovered that when a penguin has found steps going up somewhere, it is absolutely impossible to keep him from climbing them.

"All right," said Mr. Popper, panting up the steps behind Captain Cook. "I suppose, being a bird, and one

59

that can't fly, you have to go up in the air somehow, so you like to climb stairs. Well, it's a good thing this building has only three stories. Come on. Let's see what you can do."

Slowly but unwearyingly, Captain Cook lifted one pink foot after another from one step to the next, followed by Mr. Popper at the other end of the clothesline.

At last they came to the top landing.

"Now what?" inquired Mr. Popper of Captain Cook.

Finding there were no more steps to climb, Captain Cook turned around and surveyed the steps that now went down.

Then he raised his flippers and leaned forward.

Mr. Popper, who was still panting for breath, had not supposed the determined bird would plunge so quickly. He should have remembered that penguins will toboggan whenever they get a chance.

Perhaps he had been unwise in tying one end of the clothesline to his own wrist.

At any rate, this time Mr. Popper found himself suddenly sliding, on his own white-clad stomach, down the three flights of steps. This delighted the penguin, who was enjoying his own slide just ahead of Mr. Popper.

When they reached the bottom, Captain Cook was so eager to go up again that Mr. Popper had to call a taxi, to distract him.

"432 Proudfoot Avenue," said Mr. Popper to the driver.

The driver, who was a kind and polite man, did not laugh at his oddly assorted passengers until he had been paid.

"Oh dear!" said Mrs. Popper, when she opened the door to her husband. "You looked so neat and handsome when you started for your walk. And now look at the front of you!"

"I am sorry, my love," said Mr. Popper in a humble tone, "but you can't always tell what a penguin will do next."

So saying, he went to lie down, for he was quite exhausted from all the unusual exercise, while Captain Cook had a shower and took a nap in the icebox.

CHAPTER   X

Shadows

N EXT DAY the picture of Mr. Popper and Captain Cook appeared in the Stillwater *Morning Chronicle,* with a paragraph about the house painter who had received a penguin by air express from Admiral Drake in the faraway Antarctic. Then the Associated Press picked up the story, and a week later the photograph, in rotogravure, could be seen in the Sunday edition of the most important newspapers in all the large cities in the country.

Naturally the Poppers all felt very proud and happy. Captain Cook was not happy, however. He had suddenly ceased his gay, exploring little walks about the house, and would sit most of the day, sulking, in the refrigerator. Mrs. Popper had removed all the stranger objects, leaving only the marbles and checkers, so that Captain Cook now had a nice, orderly little rookery.

"He won't play with us any more," said Bill. "I tried to get some of my marbles from him, and he tried to bite me."

"Naughty Captain Cook," said Janie.

"Better leave him alone, children," said Mrs. Popper. "He feels mopey, I guess."

But it was soon clear that it was something worse than mopiness that ailed Captain Cook. All day he would sit with his little white-circled eyes staring out sadly from the refrigerator. His coat had lost its lovely, glossy look; his round little stomach grew flatter every day.

He would turn away now when Mrs. Popper would offer him some canned shrimps.

One evening she took his temperature. It was one hundred and four degrees.

"Well, Papa," she said, "I think you had better call

the veterinary doctor. I am afraid Captain Cook is really ill."

But when the veterinary came, he only shook his head. He was a very good animal doctor, and though he had never taken care of a penguin before, he knew enough about birds to see at a glance that this one was seriously ill.

"I will leave you some pills. Give him one every hour. Then you can try feeding him on sherbet and wrapping him in ice packs. But I cannot give you any encouragement because I am afraid it is a hopeless case. This kind of bird was never made for this climate, you know. I can see that you have taken good care of him, but an Antarctic penguin can't thrive in Stillwater."

That night the Poppers sat up all night, taking turns changing the ice packs.

It was no use. In the morning Mrs. Popper took Captain Cook's temperature again. It had gone up to one hundred and five.

Everyone was very sympathetic. The reporter on the *Morning Chronicle* stopped in to inquire about the pen-

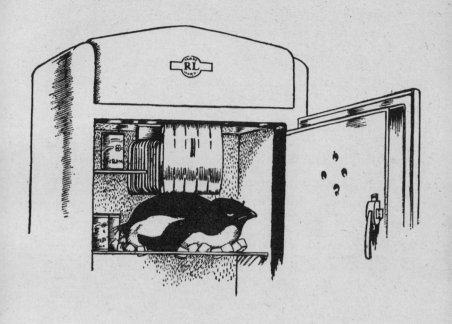

guin. The neighbors brought in all sorts of broths and
jellies to try to tempt the little fellow. Even Mrs. Callahan,
who had never had a very high opinion of Captain Cook,
made a lovely frozen custard for him. Nothing did any
good. Captain Cook was too far gone.

He slept all day now in a heavy stupor, and everyone was saying that the end was not far away.

All the Poppers had grown terribly fond of the funny, solemn little chap, and Mr. Popper's heart was frozen with terror. It seemed to him that his life would be very empty if Captain Cook went away.

Surely someone would know what to do for a sick penguin. He wished that there were some way of asking advice of Admiral Drake, away down at the South Pole, but there was not time.

In his despair, Mr. Popper had an idea. A letter had brought him his pet. He sat down and wrote another letter.

It was addressed to Dr. Smith, the Curator of the great Aquarium in Mammoth City, the largest in the world. Surely if anyone anywhere had any idea what could cure a dying penguin, this man would.

Two days later there was an answer from the Curator. "Unfortunately," he wrote, "it is not easy to cure a sick penguin. Perhaps you do not know that we too have, in our aquarium at Mammoth City, a penguin from the Antarctic. It is failing rapidly, in spite of everything we have done for it. I have wondered lately whether it is not suffering from loneliness. Perhaps that is what ails your Captain Cook. I am, therefore, shipping you, under separate cover, our penguin. You may keep her. There is just a chance that the birds may get on better together."

And that is how Greta came to live at 432 Proudfoot Avenue.

CHAPTER XI

Greta

S O CAPTAIN COOK did not die, after all.

There were two penguins in the refrigerator, one standing and one sitting on the nest under the ice cubes.

"They're as like as two peas," said Mrs. Popper.

"As two penguins, you mean," answered Mr. Popper.

"Yes, but which is which?"

At this moment the standing penguin jumped out of the icebox, reached inside and took one of the checkers from under the sitting penguin, whose eyes were closed in sleep, and laid it at Mr. Popper's feet.

"See, Mamma, he's thanking me," said Mr. Popper, patting the penguin. "At the South Pole that's the way a penguin shows its friendship, only it uses a stone instead of a checker. This one must be Captain Cook, and he's trying to show that he's grateful to us for getting him Greta and saving his life."

"Yes, but how are we going to tell them apart? It's very confusing."

"I will go down in the cellar and get some white paint and paint their names on their black backs."

And he opened the cellar door and started down, nearly tripping when Captain Cook unexpectedly tobogganed down after him. When he came up again, Mr. Popper had a brush and a small paint-can in his hands, while the penguin had a white CAPT. COOK on his back.

"*Gook!*" said Captain Cook, proudly showing his name to the penguin in the icebox.

"*Gaw!*" said the sitting Penguin, and then squirming

69

around in her nest, she turned her back to Mr. Popper.

So Mr. Popper sat down on the floor in front of the icebox, while Captain Cook watched, first with one eye, then with the other.

"What are you going to call her?" asked Mrs. Popper.

"Greta."

"It's a nice name," said Mrs. Popper, "and she seems like a nice bird, too. But the two of them fill the icebox, and pretty soon there will be eggs, and the next thing you know, the icebox won't be big enough for your penguins. Besides, you haven't done a thing about how I'm going to keep the food cold."

"I will, my love," promised Mr. Popper. "It is already pretty cold for the middle of October, and it will soon be cold enough outside for Captain Cook and Greta."

"Yes," said Mrs. Popper, "but if you keep them outside the house, they might run away."

"Mamma," said Mr. Popper, "you put your food back in the icebox tonight, and we will just keep Greta and Captain Cook in the house. Captain Cook can help me move the nest into the other room. Then I will open all the windows and leave them open, and the penguins will be comfortable."

"They will be comfortable, all right," said Mrs. Popper, "but what about us?"

"We can wear our winter overcoats and hats in the house," said Mr. Popper, as he got up to go around and open all the windows.

"It certainly is colder," said Mrs. Popper, sneezing.

The next few days were even colder, but the Poppers soon got used to sitting around in their overcoats. Greta and Captain Cook always occupied the chairs nearest the open windows.

One night, quite early in November, there was a blizzard, and when the Poppers got up in the morning, there were large drifts of snow all over the house.

Mrs. Popper wanted to get her broom and have Mr. Popper bring his snow shovel to clear away the drifts, but the penguins were having so much fun in the snow that Mr. Popper insisted it should be left where it was.

In fact, he even went so far as to bring an old garden hose up from the basement and sprinkle all the floors that night until the water was an inch deep. By the next morning all the Popper floors were covered with smooth ice, with snowdrifts around the edges near the open windows.

Both Greta and Captain Cook were tremendously pleased with all that ice. They would go up on the snowdrift at one end of the living room, and run down, one behind the other, onto the ice, until they were running too fast to keep their balance. Then they would flop on their stomachs and toboggan across the slippery ice.

This amused Bill and Janie so much that they tried it, too, on the stomachs of their overcoats. This in turn pleased the penguins greatly. Then Mr. Popper moved all the furniture in the living room to one side, so that the penguins and the children would have plenty of room for real sliding. It was a little hard at first to move the furniture, because the feet of the chairs had frozen into the ice.

Toward afternoon the weather got warmer and the ice

began to melt. "Now, Papa," said Mrs. Popper, "you really must do something. We can't go on like this."

"But Captain Cook and Greta are both fat and sleek, and the children have never been so rosy."

"It may be very healthy," said Mrs. Popper, as she mopped up the flood, "but it's very untidy."

"I will do something about it tomorrow," said Mr. Popper.

CHAPTER XII

More Mouths to Feed

S O THE NEXT DAY Mr. Popper called an engineer and had a large freezing plant installed in the cellar, and took Captain Cook and Greta down there to live. Then he had the furnace taken out and moved upstairs into the living room. It looked very odd there, but, as Mrs. Popper said, it was a relief at least not to have to wear their overcoats all the time.

Mr. Popper was quite worried when he found that all these changes were going to be very expensive. The refrigerating engineer was worried, too, when he found that Mr. Popper had practically no money. However, Mr. Popper promised to pay as soon as he could, and the man let him have everything on credit.

It was a good thing that Mr. Popper got the penguins moved when he did, because Mrs. Popper had been right about the eggs. The rookery had scarcely been moved to the basement when Greta laid the first egg. Three days later the second one appeared.

Since Mr. Popper knew that penguins lay only two eggs a season, he was astonished when, a little later, the third egg was found under Greta. Whether the change in climate had changed the penguins' breeding habits, Mr. Popper never knew, but every third day a new one would appear until there were ten in all.

Now penguin eggs are so large that the mother can sit on only two at a time, and this created quite a problem. Mr. Popper solved it, however, by distributing the extra eggs under hot-water bottles and electric heating-pads, kept just at penguin-body heat.

The penguin chicks, when they began to hatch, were
not so handsomely marked as their mother and father.
They were fuzzy, droll little creatures who grew at a

tremendous rate. Captain Cook and Greta were kept very busy bringing food to them, though, of course the Poppers all helped, too.

Mr. Popper, who had always been such a great reader, had no difficulty in thinking of names for the penguin children. They were Nelson, Columbus, Louisa, Jenny, Scott, Magellan, Adelina, Isabella, Ferdinand, and Victoria. Still, he was rather relieved that there were no more than ten to name.

Mrs. Popper, too, thought that this was about enough penguins for anybody, though they really did not make much difference to her in her housework — as long as Mr. Popper and the children remembered to close the cellar door in the kitchen.

The penguins all loved to climb the stairs that led up to the kitchen, and never knew when to stop unless they found the kitchen door closed. Then, of course, they would turn around and toboggan down the steps again. This made rather a curious noise sometimes, when Mrs. Popper was working in the kitchen, but she got used to it, as she had got used to so many other strange things this winter.

The freezing plant that Mr. Popper had got for the penguins downstairs was a large and good one. It made very large blocks of ice, instead of small ice cubes, so that soon Mr. Popper had made a sort of ice castle down there for the twelve penguins to live in and climb over.

Mr. Popper also dug a large hole in the cellar floor and made a swimming and diving pool for the birds. From time to time he would throw live fish into the pool for the penguins to dive for. They found this very refreshing, because, to tell the truth, they had got a little tired of canned shrimps. The live fish were specially ordered and were brought all the way from the coast in tank cars and glass boxes to 432 Proudfoot Avenue. Unfortunately, they were quite expensive.

It was nice that there were so many penguins because when two of them (usually Nelson and Columbus) got into a fight, and began to spar at each other with their flippers, the ten other penguins would all crowd around

78

to watch the fight and make encouraging remarks. This made a very interesting little scene.

Mr. Popper also flooded a part of the cellar floor for an ice rink, and here the penguins often drilled like a sort of small army, in fantastic marching movements and parades around the ice. The penguin Louisa seemed especially fond of leading these marching drills. It was quite a sight to see them, after Mr. Popper had the idea of training Louisa to hold a small American flag in her beak while she proudly led the solemn parades.

Janie and Bill would often bring their little friends home from school with them, and they would all go down and watch the penguins for hours.

At night, instead of sitting and reading and smoking his pipe in the living room, as he had done before, Mr. Popper would put on his overcoat and take his things downstairs. There he would sit and read, with his mittens on, looking up from time to time to see what his pets were doing. He often thought about the cold, distant regions in which the little creatures really belonged.

Often, too, he thought how different his life had been before the penguins had come to keep him occupied. It was January now, and already he dreaded to think of the time when spring would come, and he would have to leave them all day and go back to painting houses.

CHAPTER XIII

Money Worries

T HERE CAME a night, however, when Mrs. Popper, having put the children to bed, stopped Mr. Popper on his way to the cellar.

"Papa," she said, "I must talk to you. Come and sit down."

"Yes, my love," said Mr. Popper, "what is on your mind?"

"Papa," said Mrs. Popper, "I'm glad to see you having such a nice vacation. And I must say that it's been easier than usual to keep the place tidy, with you down in the basement all the time. But, Papa, what are we to do for money?"

"What is the trouble?" asked Mr. Popper.

"Well, of course, the penguins have to eat, but have you any idea what the bills for all those live fish are? I'm sure I don't know how we're ever going to pay for them. And the engineer who put in the basement freezing plant keeps ringing the doorbell and asking for his money."

"Is our money all gone?" asked Mr. Popper quietly.

"Practically all. Of course when it is all gone, maybe we could eat the twelve penguins for a while."

"Oh no, Mamma," said Mr. Popper. "You don't mean that."

"Well, I don't suppose I really could enjoy eating them, especially Greta and Isabella," said Mrs. Popper.

"It would break the children's hearts, too," said Mr. Popper. He sat there thoughtfully for quite a while.

"I have an idea, Mamma," he said at last.

"Maybe we could sell them to somebody, and then we would have a little money to live on," said Mrs. Popper.

"No," said Mr. Popper, "I have a better idea. We will keep the penguins. Mamma, you have heard of trained seals, acting in theaters?"

"Of course I have heard of trained seals," answered Mrs. Popper. "I even saw some once. They balanced balls on the ends of their noses."

"Very well then," said Mr. Popper, "if there can be trained dogs and trained seals, why can't there be trained penguins?"

"Perhaps you are right, Papa."

"Of course I am right. And you can help me train the penguins."

The next day they had the piano moved down into the basement at one end of the ice rink. Mrs. Popper had not played the piano since she had married Mr. Popper, but with a little practise she soon began to remember some of the pieces she had forgotten.

"What these penguins like to do most," said Mr. Popper, "is to drill like an army, to watch Nelson and Columbus get in a fight with each other, and to climb up steps and toboggan down. And so we will build our act around those tricks."

"They don't need costumes, anyway," said Mrs. Popper, looking at the droll little figures. "They already have a costume."

So Mrs. Popper picked out three different tunes to play on the basement piano, one for each different kind of act. Soon the penguins knew, from hearing the music, just what they were to do.

When they were supposed to parade like a lot of soldiers, Mrs. Popper played Schubert's "Military March."

When Nelson and Columbus were to fight each other with their flippers, Mrs. Popper played the "Merry Widow Waltz."

When the penguins were supposed to climb and toboggan, Janie and Bill would drag out into the middle of the ice two portable stepladders and a board that Mr. Popper had used when he was decorating houses. Then Mrs. Popper would play a pretty, descriptive piece called "By the Brook."

It was cold in the cellar, of course, so that Mrs. Popper had to learn to play the piano with her gloves on.

By the end of January, Mr. Popper was sure the penguins were ready to appear in any theater in the country.

CHAPTER XIV

Mr. Greenbaum

L OOK HERE," said Mr. Popper at breakfast one morning. "It says here in the *Morning Chronicle* that Mr. Greenbaum, the owner of the Palace Theater, is in town. He's got a string of theaters all over the country; so I guess we had better go down and see him."

That evening — it was Saturday, the twenty-ninth of January — the Popper family and their twelve trained penguins, two of them carrying flags in their beaks, left the house to find the Palace Theater.

The penguins were now so well trained that Mr. Popper decided that it was not necessary to keep them on leashes. Indeed, they walked to the bus line very nicely in the following line of march: —

Mr. Popper   Greta   Columbus   Mrs. Pop
              Captain Cook   Victoria

Nelson   Magellan   Bill Popper   Scott   Ferdinand
    Jenny   Adelina   Janie Popper   Isabella   Louisa

The bus stopped at the corner, and before the astonished driver could protest, they had all climbed on and the bus was on its way.

"Do I pay half-fare for the birds, or do they go free?" asked Mr. Popper.

"Janie goes half-fare, but I'm ten," said Bill.

"Hush," said Mrs. Popper as she and the children found their seats. The penguins followed in an orderly fashion.

"Say, mister," said the driver, "where do you think you're going with that exhibit?"

"Downtown," said Mr. Popper. "Here, let's call it fifty cents, and let it go at that."

"To tell the truth, I lost count when they went past me," said the driver.

"It's a trained penguin act," explained Mr. Popper.

"Are they really birds?" asked the driver.

"Oh yes," said Mr. Popper. "I'm just taking them down to the Palace to interview Mr. Greenbaum, the big theater owner."

"Well, if I hear any complaints, off they go at the next corner," said the driver.

"Fair enough," said Mr. Popper, who wanted to ask for transfers in that case, but decided to let well enough alone.

The penguins were behaving very well. They were sitting quietly two in a seat, while the other passengers looked on.

"Sorry," said Mr. Popper, addressing everyone in the bus, "but I'll have to open all the windows. These are Antarctic penguins and they're used to having it a lot colder than this."

It took Mr. Popper quite a while to open the windows, which were stuck fast. When he had succeeded, there were plenty of remarks from the other passengers. Many of them began to complain to the driver, who told Mr. Popper to take his birds off the bus. He had to repeat this several times. Finally he refused to take the bus any farther until Mr. Popper got off. By this time, however, the bus had got so far downtown that none of them minded having to get out into the street.

Only a block ahead of them shone the lights of the Palace Theater.

"Hello," said the theater manager, as the Poppers and the penguins trooped past him. "Sure, Mr. Greenbaum's here in my office. You know I've heard about these birds of yours, but I didn't really believe it. Mr. Greenbaum, meet the Popper Penguins. I'll be leaving you. I've got to go backstage."

The penguins, now standing politely in two rows of six each, looked curiously at Mr. Greenbaum. Their twenty-four white-circled eyes were very solemn.

"All you people crowding around the door, go back where you belong," said Mr. Greenbaum. "This is a private conference." Then he got up to shut the door.

The Poppers sat down while Mr. Greenbaum walked up and down the double row of penguins, looking them over.

"It looks like an act," he said.

"Oh, it's an act, all right," said Mr. Popper. "It's Popper's Performing Penguins, First Time on any Stage,

Direct from the South Pole." He and Mrs. Popper had thought up this name for the act.

"Couldn't we call them Popper's Pink-toed Penguins?" asked Mr. Greenbaum.

Mr. Popper thought for a moment. "No," he said, "I'm afraid we couldn't. That sounds too much like chorus girls or ballet dancers, and these birds are pretty serious. I don't think they'd like it."

"All right," said Mr. Greenbaum. "Show me the act."

"There's music to it," said Janie. "Mamma plays the piano."

"Is that true, madam?" asked Mr. Greenbaum.

"Yes, sir," answered Mrs. Popper.

"Well, there's a piano behind you," said Mr. Greenbaum. "You may begin, madam. I want to see this act. If it's any good, you people have come to the right place. I've got theaters from coast to coast. But first let's see your penguins perform. Ready, madam?"

"We'd better move the furniture first," said Bill.

CHAPTER XV

Popper's Performing Penguins

A T THAT MOMENT they were in-
terrupted by the manager, who came
in with a groan.

"What's the matter?" asked Mr.
Greenbaum.

"The Marvelous Marcos, who close the program,
haven't turned up, and the audience are demanding their
money back."

"What are you going to do?" asked Mr. Greenbaum.

"Give it to them, I suppose. And here it is Saturday
night, the biggest night of the week. I hate to think of
losing all that money."

"I have an idea," said Mrs. Popper. "Maybe you won't have to lose it. As long as it's the end of the program, why don't we just have the penguins rehearse in there on a real stage? We'd have more room, and I think the audience would enjoy it."

"All right," said the manager. "Let's try it."

So the penguins had their first rehearsal on a real stage.

The manager stepped out on the stage. "Ladies and gentlemen," he said, raising his hand, "with your kind indulgence we are going to try out a little novelty number tonight. Owing to unforeseen circumstances, the Marvelous Marcos are unable to appear. We are going to let you see a rehearsal of the Popper Performing Penguins, instead. I thank you."

In a dignified way the Poppers and the penguins walked out on the stage, and Mrs. Popper sat down at the piano.

"Aren't you going to take off your gloves to play?" asked the manager.

"Oh, no," said Mrs. Popper. "I'm so used to playing with them that I'll keep them on, if you don't mind."

Then she started Schubert's "Military March." The penguins began to drill very nicely, wheeling and changing their formations with great precision, until Mrs. Popper stopped playing in the middle of the piece.

The audience clapped vigorously.

"There's more to it," explained Mrs. Popper, half to the manager and half to the audience, "where they form in a hollow square and march in that formation. It's so late we'll skip that tonight and jump to the second part."

"You're sure you don't want to take your gloves off, madam?" asked the manager.

Mrs. Popper smilingly shook her head and began the "Merry Widow Waltz."

Ten of the penguins now formed in a semicircle as Nelson and Columbus in their midst put on a wild sparring contest. Their round black heads leaned far back so that they could watch each other with both round white eyes.

"*Gork,*" said Nelson, punching Columbus in the stomach with his right flipper, and then trying to push him over with his left flipper.

"*Gaw,*" said Columbus, going into a clinch and hanging his head over Nelson's shoulder as he tried to punch him in the back.

"Hey! No fair!" said the manager. Columbus and Nelson broke loose as the other ten penguins, looking on, applauded with their flippers.

Columbus now sparred politely with Nelson until Nelson hit him on the eye, whereupon Columbus retreated with a loud "*Ork.*" The other penguins began to clap, and the audience joined them. As Mrs. Popper finished the Waltz, both Nelson and Columbus stopped fighting, put down their flippers and stood still, facing each other.

"Which bird won? Who's ahead?" shouted the audience.

"*Gook!*" said all the ten penguins in the semicircle. This must have meant "Look!" for Nelson turned to look at them, and Columbus immediately punched him in the stomach with one flipper and knocked him down with the other. Nelson lay there, with his eyes closed.

Columbus then counted ten over the prostrate Nelson, and again the ten other penguins applauded.

"That's part of the act," explained Janie. "The other penguins all like Columbus to win, and so they all say '*Gook!*' at the end. That always makes Nelson look away, so Columbus can sock him good."

Nelson now rose to his feet, and all the penguins formed in a row, and bowed to the manager.

"Thank you," said the manager, bowing back.

"Now comes part three," said Mr. Popper.

"Oh, Papa," said Mrs. Popper. "You forgot to bring the two painting stepladders and the board!"

"That's all right," said the manager. "I'll get the stage-hands to bring some."

In no time at all a pair of ladders and a board were brought in and Mr. Popper and the children showed them how the ladders had to be set up with the board resting on top. Then Mrs. Popper began playing the pretty descriptive piece "By the Brook."

At this point in the act the penguins always forgot

their discipline and got dreadfully excited. They would all begin shoving at once to see which could be the first to climb the ladders. However, the children had always told Mr. Popper that the act was all the funnier for all this pushing and scrambling, and Mr. Popper supposed it was.

So now with a great deal of squawking the penguins fought and climbed the ladders and ran across the board in complete confusion, often knocking each other entirely off to the floor below, and then hurrying to toboggan down the other ladder and knock off any penguins who were trying to climb up there.

This part of the act was very wild and noisy in spite of Mrs. Popper's delicate music. The manager and the audience were all holding their sides, laughing.

At last Mrs. Popper got to the end of the music and took off her gloves.

"You'll have to get those ladders off the stage, or I'll never get these birds under control," said Mr. Popper. "The curtain is supposed to fall at this point."

So the manager gave the signal for the curtain to go down, and the audience stood up and cheered.

When the ladders had been taken away, the manager had twelve ice-cream cones brought in for the penguins. Then Janie and Bill began to cry, so the manager ordered several more, and everybody had one.

Mr. Greenbaum was the first to congratulate the Poppers.

"I don't mind telling you, Mr. Popper, that I think you've got something absolutely unique in those birds. Your act is a sensation. And the way you helped out my friend the manager, here, shows that you're real troupers — the kind we need in the show business. I'd like to predict that your penguins will soon be packing the biggest theaters from Oregon to Maine.

"And now to come to terms, Mr. Popper," he continued. "How about a ten-week contract at five thousand dollars a week?"

"Is that all right, Mamma?" asked Mr. Popper.

"Yes, that's very satisfactory," answered Mrs. Popper.

"Well, then," said Mr. Greenbaum, "just sign these papers. And be ready to open next Thursday in Seattle."

"And thanks again," said the manager. "Would you mind putting on your gloves again for just a minute, Mrs. Popper? I'd like you to start playing that 'Military March' again and let the penguins parade for a minute. I want to get my ushers in here to look at those birds. It would be a lesson to them."

CHAPTER XVI

On The Road

DURING THE NEXT day there was much to be done at 432 Proudfoot Avenue. There were new clothes to buy for all of them, and the old ones to pack away in moth balls. Then Mrs. Popper had to scrub and polish and straighten the whole place, for she was much too good a housekeeper to leave everything at sixes and sevens while the Poppers were away.

Mr. Greenbaum sent them their first week's pay in advance. The first thing they did was to pay off the man who had installed the freezing plant in the basement. He had been getting rather uneasy about his money; and after all, without him they could never have trained the penguins. Next they sent a check to the company who had been shipping the fresh fish all the way from the coast.

At last everything was done, and Mr. Popper turned the key in the door of the little house.

They were a little late in arriving at the railway station on account of the argument with the traffic policeman. The argument was on account of the accident to the two taxicabs.

With four Poppers and twelve penguins, not to mention the eight suitcases and pail of water with the live fish for the penguins' lunch, Mr. Popper found that they could not all fit into one cab; so he had to call a second one.

Each of the taxi-drivers was eager to be the first to get to the station and surprise the people there by opening the door of his cab and letting out six penguins. So they raced each other all the way, and in the last block they tried to pass each other, and one of the fenders got torn off.

The traffic officer naturally got very much annoyed.

The train was about to pull out of the station when they arrived. Even with both taxi-drivers helping them through the gate and over the brass rails onto the rear observation platform, they barely made it. The penguins were gasping.

It had been decided that Mr. Popper should ride in the baggage car with the penguins to keep them from getting nervous, while Mrs. Popper and the children should ride in one of the Pullmans. Because of getting on at the observation end of the train, Mr. Popper had to take the birds through the whole length of the train.

It was easy enough to get them through the club car, even with the pail of fish to carry. In the sleeping cars, however, where the porter was already making up some of the berths, there was trouble.

The porters' ladders offered too much temptation to the penguins.

There were a dozen happy *Orks* from a dozen ecstatic

beaks. Popper's Performing Penguins, completely forgetting their discipline, fought to climb the ladders and get into the upper berths.

Poor Mr. Popper! One old lady screamed that she was going to get off the train, whether it was going ninety miles an hour or not. A gentleman wearing a clergyman's collar suggested opening a window, so that the penguins could jump out. Two porters tried to shoo the birds out of the berths. Finally the conductor and the brakeman, with a lantern, came to the rescue.

It was quite a while before Mr. Popper got his pets safely into the baggage car.

Mrs. Popper worried a little, at the start, over the idea of having Janie and Bill miss ten weeks of school while they were on the road, though the children did not seem to mind.

"And you must remember, my love," said Mr. Popper, who had never before been out of Stillwater, in spite of his dreams of distant countries, "that travel is very broadening."

From the start the penguins were a riotous success. Even their opening performance in Seattle went off without a hitch — probably because they had already rehearsed on a real stage.

It was here that the penguins added a little novelty number of their own to the program. They were the first thing on the bill. When they finished their regular act, the audience went wild. They clapped and stamped and roared for more of Popper's Performing Penguins.

Janie and Bill helped their father herd the penguins off the stage, so that the next act could go on.

This next act was a tightrope walker, named Monsieur Duval. The trouble was that instead of watching him from the wings, as they should have done, the penguins got interested and walked out on the stage again to watch him more closely.

Unfortunately at this moment Monsieur Duval was doing a very difficult dance on the wire overhead.

The audience, of course, had thought that the penguins were all through, and were very much pleased to see

them return and line up with their backs to the audience and look up at Monsieur Duval, dancing so carefully on the wire high above them.

This made everyone laugh so hard that Monsieur Duval lost his balance.

"*Ork!*" said the penguins waddling away hurriedly, in order not to be under him when he fell.

Cleverly recovering his balance, Monsieur Duval caught the wire by the inside of his elbow and saved himself. He was very angry when he saw the Popper Performing Penguins opening wide their twelve red beaks, as if they were laughing at him.

"Go away, you stupid things," he said to them in French.

"*Ork?*" said the penguins, pretending not to understand, and making remarks to each other in penguin language about Monsieur Duval.

And whenever they appeared, the more they interfered with the other acts on the program the better the audiences liked them.

CHAPTER XVII

Fame

THE BIRDS soon became so famous that whenever it was known that the Popper Performing Penguins were to appear at any theater, the crowds would stand in line for half a mile down the street, waiting their turn to buy tickets.

The other actors on the program were not always so pleased, however. Once, in Minneapolis, a celebrated lady opera singer got very much annoyed when she heard that the Popper Penguins were to appear on the same program. In fact, she refused to go on the stage unless the penguins were put away. So the stage hands helped Mr. and Mrs. Popper and the children get the birds off the stage and downstairs to a basement under the stage, while the manager guarded the stage entrance to make sure that the penguins did not get past.

Down in the basement, the birds soon discovered another little flight of steps going up; and in another minute the audience was shrieking with laughter, as the penguins' heads suddenly appeared, one by one, in the orchestra pit, where the musicians were playing.

The musicians kept on playing, and the lady on the stage, when she saw the penguins, sang all the louder to show how angry she was. The audience was laughing so hard that nobody could hear the words of her song.

Mr. Popper, who had followed the penguins up the stairs, stopped when he saw that it led to the orchestra pit.

"I don't think I'm supposed to go up there with the musicians," he told Mrs. Popper.

"The penguins did," said Mrs. Popper.

"Papa, you'd better get them off before they start biting the pegs and strings off the fiddles," said Bill.

"Oh dear, I just don't know what to do," said Mr. Popper, sitting down helplessly on the top step.

"Then *I* will catch the penguins," said Mrs. Popper, climbing up past him, with Janie and Bill following.

When they saw Mrs. Popper coming after them, the penguins felt very guilty, because they knew they did not belong there. So they jumped up on the stage, ran over the footlights, and hid under the singing lady's blue skirts.

That stopped the singing entirely except for one high, shrill note that had not been written in the music.

The birds loved the bright lights of the theater, and the great, laughing audiences, and all the traveling. There was always something new to see.

From Stillwater out to the Pacific coast they traveled. It was a long way now to the little house at 432 Proudfoot Avenue, where the Poppers had had to worry about whether their money would hold out until spring.

And every week they got a check for five thousand dollars.

When they were not actually playing in some theater, or traveling on trains between cities, their life was spent in the larger hotels.

Now and then a startled hotelkeeper would object to having the birds register there.

"Why, we don't even allow lap dogs in this hotel," he would say.

"Yes, but do you have any rule against penguins?" Mr. Popper would ask.

Then the hotelkeeper would have to admit that there was no rule at all about penguins. And of course, when he saw how neat the penguins were, and how other guests came to his hotel in the hope of seeing them, he was very glad to have them. You might think that a large hotel would offer a great many opportunities for mischief to a lot of penguins, but they behaved very well, on the whole, never doing anything worse than riding up and down too often in the elevators, and occasionally biting the brass buttons off some bell-boy's uniform.

Five thousand dollars a week may sound like a great deal of money, and yet the Poppers were far from rich. It was quite expensive to live in grand hotels and travel about town in taxicabs. Mr. Popper often thought that the penguins could just as well have walked back and forth between hotels and theaters, but every one of their walks looked so much like a parade that it always tied up the traffic. So Mr. Popper, who never liked to be a nuisance to anyone, always took taxis instead.

It was expensive to have huge cakes of ice brought up to their hotel rooms, to cool the penguins. The bills in the fine restaurants where the Poppers often took their meals were often dreadfully high. Fortunately, however, the penguins' food had stopped being an expense to them. On the road, they had to give up having tank cars of live fish shipped to them, because it was so hard to get deliveries on time. So they went back to feeding the birds on canned shrimps.

This cost them absolutely nothing, for Mr. Popper had written a testimonial saying: "Popper's Performing Penguins thrive on Owens' Oceanic Shrimp."

This statement, with a picture of the twelve penguins, was printed in all the leading magazines, and the Owens Oceanic Shrimp Company gave Mr. Popper an order that was good for free cans of shrimps at any grocery store anywhere in the country.

Several other companies, such as the Great Western Spinach Growers' Association and the Energetic Breakfast Oats Company, wanted him to recommend their product, too, and offered him large sums of cash. But the penguins simply refused to eat spinach or oats, and Mr. Popper was much too honest to say they would, even though he knew the money would come in handy.

From the Pacific coast they turned east again, to cross the continent. They had time enough, on this brief tour, to touch only the larger cities. After Minneapolis, they played Milwaukee, Chicago, Detroit, Cleveland, and Philadelphia.

Wherever they went, their reputation traveled ahead of them. When, early in April, they reached Boston, huge crowds awaited them in the railway station.

Up to now, it had not been too difficult to keep the

penguins comfortable. But a warm spring wind was blowing across Boston Common, and at the hotel Mr. Popper had to have the ice brought up to his rooms in thousand-pound cakes. He was glad that the ten-week contract was almost up, and that the next week, when his birds were to appear in New York, was the last.

Already Mr. Greenbaum was writing about a new contract. Mr. Popper was beginning to think, however, that he had better be getting back to Stillwater, for the penguins were growing irritable.

CHAPTER XVIII

April Winds

I F IT WAS unseasonably warm in Boston, it was actually hot in New York. In their rooms at the great Tower Hotel, overlooking Central Park, the penguins were feeling the heat badly.

Mr. Popper took them up to the roof garden to catch whatever cool breeze might be blowing. The penguins were all charmed by the sparkling lights and the confusion of the city below. The younger birds began crowding over to the edge of the roof and looking down at the great canyons beneath them. It made Mr. Popper very nervous to see them shoving each other, as if at any moment they might succeed in pushing one over. He remembered how the South Pole penguins always did this to find out what danger lay below.

The roof was not a safe place for them. Mr. Popper had never forgotten how badly frightened he had been when Captain Cook had been so ill, before Greta came. He could not risk the chance of losing one of his penguins now.

Where the penguins were concerned, nothing was ever too much trouble for him. He took them downstairs again and bathed them under the cold showers in the bathroom. This kept him busy a large part of the night.

With all this lack of sleep, he was quite drowsy the next morning when he had to call the taxis to get to the theater. Besides, Mr. Popper had always been a little absent-minded. That is how he made his great mistake when he said to the first taxi-driver: —

"Regal Theater."

"Yes, sir," said the driver, threading his way in and

out the traffic of Broadway, which greatly interested both the children and the penguins.

They had almost reached the theater, when the driver suddenly turned. "Say," he said, "you don't mean to say those penguins are going to be on the same bill with Swenson's Seals, do you?"

"I don't know what else is on the bill," said Mr. Popper, paying him. "Anyway, here's the Regal." And they piled out and filed in the stage entrance.

In the wings stood a large, burly, red-faced man. "So these are the Popper Performing Penguins, huh?" he said. "Well, I want to tell you, Mr. Popper, that I'm Swen Swenson, and those are my seals in there on the stage now, and if your birds try any funny business, it'll be too bad for them. My seals are tough, see? They'd think nothing of eating two or three penguins apiece."

From the stage could be heard the hoarse barks of the seals, who were going through their act.

"Papa," said Mrs. Popper, "the penguins are the last act on the bill. You go run back quick and get those taxis and we'll let the penguins ride around a while until it's time for their number."

Mr. Popper hurried out to catch the drivers.

When he returned, it was too late. The Popper Performing Penguins had already discovered the Swenson Seals.

"Papa, I can't look!" cried the children.

There was a sound of dreadful confusion on the stage, the audience was in an uproar, and the curtain was quickly rung down.

When the Poppers rushed onto the stage, both penguins and seals had found the stairway leading to the Swenson dressing-room and were on their way upstairs.

"I can't bear to think what's happening up there," said Mr. Popper, with a shudder.

Mr. Swenson only laughed. "I hope your birds were insured, Popper," he said. "How much were they worth? Well, let's go up and look."

"You go up, Papa," said Mrs. Popper. "Bill, you run out of the theater and call the police to come and try to save some of our penguins."

"I'll go get the fire department," said Janie.

When the firemen, with a great clanging, came and set up their ladders so that they could get in through the window of Mr. Swenson's dressing room, they were a little vexed to find that there was no fire at all. However, when they found six black-mustached seals, sitting barking in the middle of the room, with twelve penguins parading gaily around them in a square, they felt better.

Then the policemen came in their patrol, and climbed up the ladder which the firemen had left against the building. By the time they too came through the window, they could scarcely believe their eyes. For the firemen had put firemen's helmets on the penguins, which made the delighted birds look very silly and girlish.

Seeing the firemen so friendly with the penguins, the policemen naturally took sides with the seals and put policemen's caps on them. The seals looked very fierce, with their long black mustaches and black faces underneath.

The penguins under their firemen's helmets were parading in front of the policemen, while the seals, in their

policemen's caps, were barking at the firemen, when Mr. Popper and Mr. Swenson finally opened the door.

Mr. Popper sat down. His relief was so great that for a moment he could not speak.

"You policemen had better get your hats off my seals now," said Mr. Swenson. "I got to go down on the stage and finish the act now." Then he and his six seals slipped out of the room, with a few parting barks.

"Well, good-bye, ducks," said the firemen, regretfully removing their helmets from the penguins and putting them on their own heads. Then they disappeared down the ladder. The penguins, of course, wanted to follow, but Mr. Popper held them back.

Just then the door flew open, and the theater manager burst into the room.

"Hold that man," he shouted to the policemen, pointing at Mr. Popper. "I have a warrant for his arrest."

"Who, me?" said Mr. Popper, in a daze. "What have I done?"

"You've broken into my theater and thrown the place into a panic, that's what you've done. You're a disturber of the peace."

121

"But I'm Mr. Popper, and these are my Performing Penguins, famous from coast to coast."

"I don't care who you are, you haven't any business in my theater."

"But Mr. Greenbaum is going to pay us five thousand dollars for a week at the Regal."

"Mr. Greenbaum's theater is the Royal, not the Regal. You've come to the wrong theater. Anyway, out you go, you and your Performing Penguins. The patrol is waiting outside."

CHAPTER XIX

Admiral Drake

S O MR. POPPER, with Captain Cook, Greta, Columbus, Louisa, Nelson, Jenny, Magellan, Adelina, Scott, Isabella, Ferdinand, and Victoria, was bundled into the patrol wagon and hustled off to the police station.

None of his pleas could move the desk sergeant.

"That theater manager is pretty mad at the way you busted into his theater, so I'm holding you. I'm going to give you all a nice quiet cell — unless you furnish bail. I'm putting the bail at five hundred dollars for you and one hundred dollars for each of the birds."

Of course Mr. Popper did not have that much money about him. Neither did Mrs. Popper when they telephoned her at the hotel. The hotel bill was paid for several days ahead, but she had no cash. The check for the final week's salary was not due until the end of the week. Indeed, it now looked as if the Poppers would never see that check, since they could not get the penguins out of jail long enough to put on their act at the Royal Theater.

If only they could have got in touch with Mr. Greenbaum, Mr. Popper knew, that kind man would have got them out. But Mr. Greenbaum was somewhere in Hollywood, out on the Pacific Coast, and the Poppers had no idea how to reach him.

It was very dull for the birds in jail. Wednesday came and there was still no word from Mr. Greenbaum. Thursday, and the birds began to droop. It was soon apparent that the lack of exercise, combined with the heat, might prove too much for them. There were no more tricks or merry games. Even the younger birds sat all day in dismal silence, and Mr. Popper could not cheer them up.

Mr. Popper had a feeling that Mr. Greenbaum would probably turn up by the end of the week, to see about renewing the contract. But Friday passed, without any news of him.

Saturday morning Mr. Popper got up very early and smoothed his hair. Then he dusted off the penguins as well as he could, for he wanted everything to look as presentable as possible, in case Mr. Greenbaum should appear.

About ten o'clock there was a sound of footsteps in the corridor, and a jingling of keys, and the door of the cell was opened.

"You're free, Mr. Popper. There's a friend of yours here."

Mr. Popper stepped out into the light with the penguins.

"You're barely in time, Mr. Greenbaum," he was about to say.

Then, as his eyes became accustomed to the light, he looked again.

126

It was not Mr. Greenbaum who stood there.

It was a great, bearded man in a splendid uniform. Smiling, he held out his hand to Mr. Popper.

"Mr. Popper," he said, "I am Admiral Drake."

"Admiral Drake!" gasped Mr. Popper. "Not back from the South Pole!"

"Yes," said the Admiral, "the Drake Antarctic Expedition ship returned yesterday. You should have seen the reception New York gave us. You can read about it in today's paper. But I read about the trouble you were having over the penguins, and so here I am. I have a long story to tell you."

"Could we go to the hotel and talk about it?" asked Mr. Popper. "My wife will be anxious to see us back."

"Certainly," said the Admiral. And when they were all settled in the Popper rooms at the hotel, with the penguins clustering round to listen, Admiral Drake began: —

"Naturally, when I knew that I was coming back to America, I often thought about the man to whom I had sent the penguin. It takes us a long time to hear things, down there, and I often wondered how you and the bird were getting along. Last night, at the Mayor's dinner for us, I heard about the wonderful trained penguin act you had been putting on all over the country. This morning I picked up the paper, and the first thing I read was that Mr. Popper and his twelve penguins were still being held in jail. But *twelve* penguins, Mr. Popper — how on earth — "

Then Mr. Popper told how Greta had arrived to keep Captain Cook from being lonely, and how the little penguins had grown, and how the clever little band had saved the day for the Poppers, when things looked bad.

"It's amazing," said Admiral Drake. "I've seen a lot of penguins in my time, but never such educated ones as these. It certainly shows what patience and training can do.

"But now to get to my real point, Mr. Popper. You probably know that I have explored the North Pole as well as the South Pole?"

"Oh yes," said Mr. Popper respectfully, "I have read

books about both your Arctic and your Antarctic expeditions."

"Well, then," said the Admiral, "maybe you know why we explorers prefer the South Pole?"

"Could it be on account of the penguins, sir?" asked Janie, who had been listening very hard.

Admiral Drake patted her head. "Yes, my dear. Those long Polar nights get pretty dull when you have no pets to play with. Of course, there are polar bears up there, but you can't play with *them*. Nobody knows why there are no penguins at the North Pole. For a long time the United States Government has been wanting me to lead an expedition up there for the purpose of establishing a breed of penguins. I must come to the point, Mr. Popper. You've had such remarkable success with these birds of yours, why not let me take them to the North Pole and start a race of penguins there?"

Just then Mr. Greenbaum and another gentleman were announced. They shook hands all around and were introduced to the Admiral.

"Well, Popper," said Mr. Greenbaum, "too bad about

that mix-up over the theaters. But never mind. Here's Mr. Klein, who owns the Colossal Film Company. He's going to make your fortune. You'll be a poor man no longer, Mr. Popper."

"Poor!" said Mr. Popper, "I'm not poor. These birds have been earning us five thousand dollars a week."

"Oh, five thousand dollars," said Mr. Klein. "What's that? Pin money. I want to put those birds in the movies, Mr. Popper. We've got the story department working on stories for them already. Why, I'll put each of those birds under a contract that will keep you and the missus on Easy Street the rest of your lives."

"Papa," whispered Mrs. Popper, "I don't want to live on Easy Street. I want to go back to Proudfoot Avenue."

"Better consider, Mr. Popper," said the Admiral. "I can't offer you anything like that."

"You say those men at the North Pole get lonely because there are no penguins?" asked Mr. Popper.

"Very lonely," said the Admiral.

"But if there were penguins up there, mightn't the polar bears eat them?"

"Oh, ordinary penguins, yes," said the Admiral judiciously; "but not such highly-trained birds as yours, Mr. Popper. They could outwit any polar bear, I guess."

It was now Mr. Klein's turn to speak.

"In every moving picture house in America little children would have the pleasure of seeing stories acted by the Popper Performing Penguins," he said.

"Of course if we succeeded in establishing the breed at the North Pole," said the Admiral, "the name might have to be changed a little. I imagine that hundreds of years from now scientists would be calling them the Popper Arctic Penguins."

Mr. Popper was silent for a moment.

"Gentlemen," he said, "I want to thank you both. I'll give you my decision tomorrow."

CHAPTER XX

Farewell, Mr. Popper

I T WAS A hard decision to make. Long after the visitors had gone, Mr. and Mrs. Popper sat and discussed what was best for everybody. Mrs. Popper could see the advantages of both offers, and she pointed these out, without trying to influence him.

"I feel that the penguins are really your responsibility," she said, "and you must make up your mind."

It was a pale and haggard Mr. Popper who was ready to announce his decision the next day.

"Mr. Klein," he said, "I want you to know how much I appreciate your offer of putting my birds in the movies. But I am afraid I have to refuse. I do not believe the life in Hollywood would be good for the penguins."

Then he turned to Admiral Drake. "Admiral Drake, I am going to give you the birds. In doing this, I am considering the birds first of all. I know that they have been comfortable and happy with me. Lately, though, with the excitement and the warm weather, I've been worried about them. The birds have done so much for me that I have to do what is best for them. After all, they belong in a cold climate. And then I can't help being sorry for those men up at the North Pole, without any penguins to help them pass the time."

"Your Government will thank you, Mr. Popper," answered the Admiral.

"Congratulations, Admiral," said Mr. Klein. "Maybe you're right at that, Popper. Hollywood might have been too much for the birds. I wish you'd let me make one short movie of them here in New York, though, before they go. Just some pictures of the sort of thing they do on the stage, you know. We'd show the film everywhere with an announcement that these are the famous Popper Penguins that are being taken to the North Pole by Admiral Drake of the United States Arctic Penguin Founding Expedition, or something like that."

"I'd like that very much," said Mr. Popper.

"We'd pay you, of course," continued Mr. Klein. "Not a fortune, as we could have if you'd let us give them a contract, but, say, twenty-five thousand dollars."

"We could use it," said Mrs. Popper.

"It will be very quiet at 432 Proudfoot Avenue," said Mr. Popper, when everyone had left.

Mrs. Popper did not answer. She knew that nothing she could say could really comfort him.

"However," said Mr. Popper, "now that spring is here, a lot of people will be wanting their houses painted, so we'd better be getting back."

"Anyway," said Bill, "we've had ten whole weeks of vacation right in the middle of the year, and not many children in Stillwater can say that."

The next day the cameramen arrived to make the picture of the penguins doing their tricks. It was arranged that the Poppers should stay in New York just long enough to see the Expedition off.

Meanwhile, in the harbor, the great sailing ship of Admiral Drake was being made ready for its long trip north. Every day huge boxes of supplies of all sorts were hustled on board. The most comfortable quarters on the ship were turned over to the penguins, who were the cause of the voyage.

Captain Cook was already quite familiar with the ship, since it was the same one the Admiral had sailed to the South Pole, where Captain Cook had often seen it. Greta, too, had seen vessels of its kind. The two of them were kept very busy showing and explaining everything to Nelson, Columbus, Louisa, Jenny, Scott, Magellan, Adelina, Isabella, Ferdinand, and Victoria.

The sailors all took the greatest delight in watching the curious little birds at their explorations.

"It looks as if this will be a pretty lively trip," they

would say. "These Popper Penguins certainly live up to their reputation."

But at last everything was ready, and the day came when the Poppers were to go down and say good-by. Bill and Janie ran all over the ship, and did not want to leave when it was time to draw up the gangplank. The Admiral shook hands with them and Mrs. Popper, and thanked them for having helped to train the extraordinary penguins that were to be a real contribution to science.

Mr. Popper had gone down below to say a private farewell to his birds. All that kept him from breaking down completely was the knowledge that what he was doing was best for them, too. First he said good-by to all the younger penguins. Then to Greta, who had saved Captain Cook. Then, last of all, he leaned over and said a special good-by to Captain Cook, who had come and made life so different for Mr. Popper.

Then he wiped his eyes, straightened his back, and went up on deck to say good-by to Admiral Drake.

"Good-by, Admiral Drake," he said.

"Good-by?" repeated the Admiral. "Why, what do you mean? Aren't you coming with us?"

"Me — go with you to the North Pole?"

"Why, of course, Mr. Popper."

"But how could I go with you? I'm not an explorer or a scientist. I'm only a house painter."

"You're the keeper of the penguins, aren't you?" roared the Admiral. "Man alive, aren't those penguins the reason for this whole Expedition? And who's going to see that they're well and happy if you're not along? Go put on one of those fur suits, like the rest of us. We're pulling anchor in a minute."

"Mamma," shouted Mr. Popper to Mrs. Popper, who had already gone up the gangplank, "I'm going, too! I'm going, too! Admiral Drake says he needs me. Mamma, do you mind if I don't come home for a year or two?"

"Oh, as to that," said Mrs. Popper, "I'll miss you very much, my dear. But we have money to live on for a few years. And in winter it will be much easier to keep the

138

house tidy without a man sitting around all day. I'll be getting back to Stillwater. Tomorrow is the day for the meeting of the Ladies' Aid and Missionary Society, and I'll be just in time. So good-by, my love, and good luck."

"Good-by and good luck!" echoed the children.

And the penguins, hearing their voices, scuttled up on deck and stood there beside the Admiral and Mr. Popper. Then they solemnly lifted their flippers and waved, as the great ship moved slowly down the river toward the sea.

THE END